The Adventures of Ale and Ju

The Friendship

LJ Sewi and NK Cola

Illustrations by NK Cola

1st Edition

Published September 2023

DEDICATION

We dedicate this book to our lovely parents - Tania and Filipe - for all the nights spent reading us stories. We also dedicate to our baby brother and sister - Ale and Ju - who inspired us to create these characters.

In this first book, Ale meets Ju, and they quickly become friends.

It's a story about how they met and how wonderful it is to have a good friend.

This is the beginning of many exciting adventures to come.

The Two

In a land where laughter's always near,
Lived Ju the piglet, full of cheer.
With feathers fine and neck so long,
Was Ale the ostrich, singing a song.

Meeting by the stream

One sunny day, by a sparkling stream,
Ju and Ale met, it seemed like a dream.
"Let's go on an adventure," Ju said with glee,
"To a place full of wonders, just you and me!"

The Enchanted Forest

Through the woods they strolled so free,

In the Enchanted Forest, a magical spree.

Twinkling fireflies led the way,

As Ju and Ale laughed and played all day.

The Great Hill Climb

They came upon a hill so high,
"Let's climb to the top, touch the sky!"
Up they went, step by step,
Helping each other, there was no misstep.

Giggles in the Meadow

At the hill's peak, what a sight to see,
A meadow of flowers, buzzing with glee.
Ju and Ale danced, oh what fun,
Their laughter echoed with the setting sun.

Splish-Splash in the River

Downhill they raced, with hearts so light,
To the river's edge, sparkling and bright.
With a splash and a jump, they both dived in,
Ripples of joy, their adventure would win.

Lost in the Maze

In a maze they wandered, paths intertwined,
Giggles turned to puzzled minds.
But together they solved the tricky maze,
Finding their way out with friendship's blaze.

Underneath the Rainbow Sky

As evening painted the sky so wide,
A rainbow appeared, with colors to guide.
Hand in hand, they made a vow,
To explore together, forever, somehow.

Bedtime Tales

Back home in their cozy den,

Ju and Ale cuddled, adventure's end.

With dreams of magic and laughter anew,

They drifted to sleep, their bond ever true.

The End

And so our tale of friendship grand,

With Ju and Ale, hand in hand.

Adventure, laughter, a bond that won't die,

Children 'round the world, reaching for the sky.

In their hearts, Ju and Ale forever fly.

ABOUT THE AUTHORS

This book was written by LJ Sewi and NK Cola. You may not find it surprising, but these two youngsters woke up one day with an idea, and this idea eventually transformed into a plan, and that plan evolved into a book. The very book you now hold in your hands.

As many of you may be aware, writing a book is no simple feat, especially for young authors who grapple with the constant demands of schoolwork and young life's other challenges.*Crafting this book was undoubtedly a formidable undertaking, one that demanded their dedication and passion. However, this does not diminish the fact that it was an enjoyable task! Creating the story, the rhymes, and even the illustrations infused warmth and imagination into every facet of this book.

NK Cola and LJ Sewi drew inspiration from their younger siblings at home, translating what they observed into the reality you see before you today. It was undeniably challenging, and no one can deny that fact. Yet, instead of giving up, they transformed these hardships into emotions and ideas that now flow through these pages. These two children transformed an idea into reality, never losing hope, even when the path to their goal seemed obscured.

I hope that as you open the enchanting pages of "Ale and Ju," it may fill you with the same joy and wonder that the making of this book has brought to them.

This unique series is a groundbreaking feat in children's literature, growing in complexity alongside the evolving ages of its young readers.

Sewi, don't forget to cross this off

* like doing what their parents tell them to do without complaining!

Printed in Great Britain
by Amazon

33713934R00016